The Haunted Mobile

Robert Dodds

For Elpy

First published 2011 by A & C Black
an imprint of Bloomsbury Publishing Plc
50 Bedford Square, London WC1B 3DP

www.acblack.com

Copyright © 2011 Robert Dodds
Illustrations copyright © 2011 Jo Bird

The rights of Robert Dodds and Jo Bird to be identified
as the author and illustrator of this work have been asserted by them
in accordance with the Copyrights, Designs and Patents Act 1988.

ISBN 978-14081-4258-5

A CIP catalogue for this book is available from the British Library.

This book is produced using paper that is made from wood
grown in managed, sustainable forests. It is natural, renewable
and recyclable. The logging and manufacturing processes conform
to the environmental regulations of the country of origin.

Printed and bound in Great Britain
by CPI Cox and Wyman, Reading, RG1 8EX

THE
HAUNTED
MOBILE

Contents

Chapter 1

Text Message

It started with a text on Jake's mobile.

```
Cold.  Dark.  Cold.
Dark.  I can't get out.
```

Jake stared at the screen. He scrolled down to see who had sent the text. It had come from his own number.

The phone was very cold in his hands. He stared at it as if it had a life of its own.

"Get a grip, Jake," he said to himself. The message must have come from his friend Roddy as a joke. Roddy was clever with phones. Jake decided to ignore the text and see what happened.

*　*　*

"Have you gone mad?" Roddy said to him at the bus stop after school. It was dark, and rain dripped onto them through a hole in the shelter.

"What?" Jake said.

"That text you sent me." Roddy showed him his screen.

```
Cold, so cold, so cold,
so cold
```

"I didn't send that," Jake said.

Roddy scrolled down. It said:

```
Message from Jake
```

Jake took out his phone.

"My mobile is doing something weird," he said. "Look at this."

He went to show Roddy the strange message in his inbox. But it wasn't there!

Jake stared at his screen. He felt sure that Roddy had done something to his phone. But why? It was a mean thing to do. Jake was glad when Roddy's bus came.

* * *

That night, Jake couldn't sleep. What was going on? Who had sent those texts? The question went around and around in his head, keeping him awake.

Outside, it was pouring with rain and Jake could hear thunder. It was a bit scary, so when his phone bleeped loudly, Jake nearly jumped out of his skin.

It was midnight. Was Roddy playing another joke? Jake picked up his phone and stared at the screen.

```
I'm so cold and scared.
Help me.  Alice
```

Alice? He didn't know anyone called Alice. He scrolled down and felt a shiver run down his spine. The message had come from his own number again.

The screen was still lit.

Delete message?

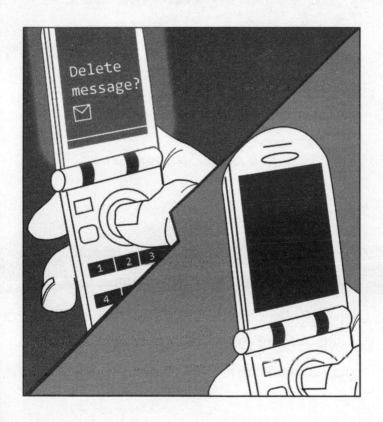

As Jake watched, the phone deleted the message all by itself, and then its screen went dark. He turned it off and put it in a drawer.

Jake lay back in his bed. Who had sent that message? Who was Alice? What was going on?

* * *

When at last Jake fell asleep, he had a disturbing dream. He was in a dark, cold place and he could hear the sound of dripping water. A lot of girls were standing with their backs towards him.

14

He went up to them one by one, and tapped them on the shoulder, saying "Are you Alice?" But as he tapped each girl she crumbled into dust, until he was standing alone, up to his ankles in soft, grey ashes.

Chapter 2

Going Mad

In the morning, the TV news was all about floods.

"It's a good job we live in this part of town!" his mum said. "Just look at all those poor people who live near the river. They all have to leave their homes!"

It rained all day. In the lunch break, everyone was crowded into the dining hall and the gym. Jake saw Roddy showing their friend Izzy something on his phone.

"Look! Here he is!" Jake heard Roddy say as he went up to them. They both gave him an odd look.

Roddy held out his mobile. Jake read the screen.

```
Are you there?  Are you
reading this?  I'm so
cold.  Help me.
```

Then Roddy scrolled down.

"Why were you sending me a message at that time of night?" Roddy asked crossly.

"It wasn't me!" said Jake. "Two o'clock in the morning? I was asleep."

Roddy looked really angry. "I've had enough of this," he said. "What's going on?"

"I don't know," said Jake. "I didn't send that message."

Roddy gave Jake a long look. Then he shook his head, and walked away.

Jake turned to Izzy. "You believe me, don't you?"

Izzy looked around.

"Roddy thinks you've gone a bit funny in the head," she said softly.

"He told me that when you were a little kid you used to see weird things, and your parents were worried about you," she said.

Jake went red. How could Roddy, his friend, tell other people about that?

When he and Roddy were at primary school, he'd told Roddy that sometimes he saw strange white-faced children staring out at him from dark places. Sometimes he could hear them calling him.

His parents said it was all in his mind and as Jake got older, he stopped seeing the white-faced children.

Now he wished he'd never told Roddy about them.

"I'm not making stuff up, Izzy," he said.

But in his mind he wasn't so sure. Had he really got those strange texts? No one else had seen them.

Could he be sending texts to Roddy without knowing it, maybe in his sleep?

But he knew his phone had been off all night and he had only switched it back on in the morning. Could he have turned it on in the night without knowing?

Did his mobile phone have a mind of its own, or was he going mad? He didn't know which was more scary.

Chapter 3

Voice Message

"More floods!" his mum said when Jake got home. She pointed at the TV. There were people being rescued in boats. A fireman climbed up a tree to rescue a cat.

The news said the town had flooded many times before. In the worst flood, fifty years ago, a whole family had been swept away by the rising water. It was all a bit sad, so Jake went to his room to read a book.

At bedtime, he fell asleep quickly. He had a dream about hands knocking at doors. He felt that someone was trying to get to him.

* * *

There was a ringing sound. He woke up with a start.

His mobile really was ringing, but by the time he'd got his hand onto it, it had stopped. He stared at the glowing screen.

`Voice message`

Jake called his voicemail and waited. It was a girl's voice, but he didn't know her.

Could it be Alice?

He couldn't hear the message very well because there was a kind of "ssshhh...." sound in the background, like running water.

"I'm sorry you... answer me... I... very cold... lonely... will you come to me... try again... so dark and cold..."

Jake listened to the message again, but he couldn't make out the missing words. He scrolled down to see the girl's number, and his heart thumped. Once again, the message had come from his own phone.

Delete voice message?

Jake pressed the Save button as quickly as he could. He needed to let people hear the voice message to prove he wasn't going crazy. But he wasn't quick enough.

Voice message deleted.

His mobile was as cold as a block of ice. He threw it down in anger and rubbed his fingers to get them warm. How was he going to prove that there had ever been a voice mail? Who would believe him?

Chapter 4

The Call

The next day was it was still raining. Jake wondered if Roddy would accuse him of sending more strange texts, but Roddy didn't speak to him all day. Jake was fed up.

By the time he was walking up his street from the bus stop, it was as dark as night. He had his hood up, but he still got soaked. The road was like a stream and the gutter was full of swirling water. Jake couldn't wait to get home and change into dry clothes and sit by the fire with some tea and toast.

His mobile rang.

"Hello, it's Jake," he said. He hoped it would be a call from one of his mates.

"Jake…"

It was the girl again. Jake could hear the water in the background.

"Is that Alice?" Jake said.

"Yes. Where are you?"

"I'm walking up Mill Street," he said.

"I want to see you. Jake, will you come to me?"

Jake wanted to get home, but the girl sounded so keen to see him. He didn't feel he could let her down.

"Where are you?" he said.

"I'm very close. Come down Mill Street towards the river. Then go left along Lane End."

"But…" Jake said.

The phone clicked off.

He had been going to ask why Alice wanted to meet in a place like Lane End. It was a dead end, with lots of empty factories. But it didn't matter. The main thing was that if he went to meet this girl, then the mystery would be solved.

He felt great that he had at last spoken to Alice. She wasn't someone he had made up. He wasn't going mad.

All those weird texts must be his phone going wrong. He would ask Mum to get him a new one.

Maybe Alice was a girl from his school. Maybe she fancied him. Things were looking up.

He could see the lights of his house just a bit further up the road. He wanted to get home and get warm. But Alice was waiting for him, so he turned back down the hill into the cold and darkness.

Chapter 5

Trapped

When Jake got to Lane End he began to think someone was playing a trick on him. There were no lights in the street, and he kept stepping in deep puddles of icy water.

Surely Alice couldn't be here? The only good thing was that the rain was not so heavy. Jake looked up and saw the moon breaking through a gap in the clouds.

Suddenly his phone rang again. Jake took it out of his pocket. It was nice to see its little glowing light in the darkness.

"Alice?"

"I know where you are."

Jake thought that was an odd thing to say. He could hear the sound of rushing water over the phone.

"Where are you?" he asked. He looked around. Could she be watching him?

"Can you see the storm drain?" Alice said.

"What's a storm drain?"

"Along the gutter, there's a hole, where rain-water can run away," said Alice.

Jake looked along the gutter.

There was a large hole with a thick iron grate over it. Rain-water was pouring down the hole and splashing down below.

"Yes, I can see it," he said.

"Lift the grate. It's very heavy, but it's just resting on top of the hole."

"Why should I do that?" asked Jake.

"Because I'm trapped down here, Jake.
I need you to help me."

Jake stared in horror down the black hole.

"I'm not going down there!" he said.

"Jake! You're my only hope!"

Alice sounded like she was going to cry.

"But how did you get down there?" he asked.

"I was swept down by the floods. Not here. From a street where there wasn't a grate."

"Alice – call 999. The police will come and get you."

"I can't! I can only call you."

It didn't make sense. Alice must have a phone – she was speaking to him. Then he had another idea.

"No worries!" he said. "I'll call 999 from my phone."

He ended the call before she could reply, and pressed 999.

There was nothing. No ring tone, nothing. He tried again, then he tried his home number, but his mobile had gone dead.

Could the rain have made his phone stop working? Now what was he going to do?

At least he should move the grate.

Perhaps Alice could climb out – if she really *was* in there.

He bent over and grabbed the wet iron grate. He pulled hard and it moved.

Chapter 6

Storm Drain

Bit by bit Jake dragged the grate away from the hole. At first he couldn't see what was down there. But then the moon came out from behind the clouds, and he saw a shaft going down about ten metres.

At the bottom of the shaft, water was rushing towards the river. A rusty iron ladder was fixed to the side of the shaft, going as far as a ledge just above the water.

Jake's phone rang. He tried to answer it, but his hands were so cold that his phone slipped from his fingers and fell down the shaft. It landed on the ledge.

It stopped ringing and Jake heard Alice's voice coming up the shaft. His mobile must have switched onto speaker mode when it fell.

"Jake? Please, Jake, answer me!"

She sounded so upset. He couldn't just walk away and leave her. He leaned over the shaft and called down.

"Alice, I've dropped my phone. But I'm coming to get it."

He tried to sound brave but he didn't feel very brave.

But if he could just get his phone back, he could talk to Alice and try to call the police again.

Jake's heart thumped as he slowly climbed down the ladder. He held the handrail tightly, until he was just above the running water.

Suddenly, with a horrible noise, the ladder above him broke away from the wall of the shaft.

Jake was swung out over the water. There was a sharp crack, and the top of the ladder snapped and fell, just missing his head.

The piece of the ladder that he was holding on to got closer and closer to the water. Jake tried to grab hold of the ledge, but the bricks were too wet and his fingers found nothing to grip.

He sank into the fast-moving stream until his feet touched the bottom. The water was freezing cold and came up to his waist.

"Jake? Are you in the water?"

Alice's voice rang out in the tunnel from his phone. Jake grabbed it off the ledge.

"The ladder broke!" he said. "Now what can I do? I can't get back up!"

He was beginning to panic but Alice's voice was full of hope.

"You're so close now! Just come along the tunnel, towards the river. I'll ring when you're near."

The phone went dead once more. He tried 999 and his mum's number again, but no luck.

He couldn't climb back up the shaft. He couldn't walk against the flow of the water, it was much too strong. The only thing he could do was follow the tunnel towards the river, just as Alice had said.

Chapter 7

Alice

It was freezing and dark in the tunnel. As he made his way along he pressed his mobile to bring the screen to life. By its dim light Jake could see the wet bricks and the swirling water.

After a bit, he heard a roaring sound ahead. Then he came to a corner, and by the light of his phone he saw that his tunnel was joining a much larger one.

The water in the larger tunnel was flowing even faster. How could he keep going?

His phone rang again. It was still on speaker, and Alice's voice filled the darkness.

"Turn left along the big tunnel, Jake. You're really close now. You can help me, I know you can."

The phone went dead again. Jake felt so cold he could hardly move his feet, but he couldn't go back. He stepped out into the bigger tunnel.

At once, the rapid flow of water knocked him over and swept him along. The dirty water went up his nose and in his mouth. He tried to grab hold of the wet bricks of the tunnel.

At last he managed to stand. The water was almost up to his chest, and pushed him forward.

Now Jake could hear something above the rushing water that set his teeth on edge. It sounded like something scraping. What was making that horrible noise?

He came to a small wall sticking out from the side of the tunnel and grabbed hold of it. He stared ahead.

Could he see something white where the scraping noise came from?

It was still pitch dark where Jake was, but there was some light at the end of the tunnel.

"The water flows into the river," thought Jake, "so that must be moonlight from outside."

He thought he could see someone standing with the light behind them. Were they waving to him?

"Alice?" he called, and his voice echoed in the tunnel.

Then the moon shone more brightly, and Jake's mouth opened in a silent scream of horror.

At the end of the tunnel was a thick iron grille. Bobbing up and down in the water against the grille, as if trying to fight its way out to the river, was a skeleton. Its white bones rubbed against the metal bars, making the harsh scraping sound. The skeleton was about his own size.

At that moment, the water turned the skeleton's head towards him, and its jaw dropped open as if in a grin.

From his mobile, Jake heard Alice's voice.

"Jake! I knew you'd make it. I'm so glad you've found me!"

Jake shook with cold and fear. The skeleton's empty eye sockets stared straight at him.

"Who are you?" he gasped. "Who's speaking?"

"Alice. I'm Alice."

"What do you want?" Jake croaked.

"My foot is caught in the bars under the water. I've been trying for fifty years to get it free. Help me, Jake!"

The skeleton's jaw opened and closed as the flowing water pushed it up and down.

In a panic Jake tried to turn back. But his feet were knocked from under him by the water, and he was swept up against the grille.

Bony fingers seemed to grab him. One of his
feet got caught in the bars of the grille under
the water and was held there in an icy grip.

Jake couldn't fight any more. He felt as if his blood was turning to ice. The water pushed the skeleton's arms around him, as if in a hug, and the grinning skull rested on his shoulder.

The voice from the phone echoed in the tunnel.

"I'm sorry, Jake. I've been so lonely. Now at least we've got each other..."

Chapter 8

Afterwards

Later on, Roddy felt bad that he had not replied to the strange texts that he kept getting in those first days when Jake didn't appear at school.

```
Water... I can't breathe
anymore... cold... I'm with
Alice now... dark forever...
```

Roddy deleted them as soon as they arrived. He felt fed up with Jake for sending them, and after a few days the texts stopped.

Then, when he found out that Jake wasn't just off school but had gone missing on the night of the floods, Roddy felt sick. He called and texted Jake, hoping for a reply, hoping that he wasn't too late.

But Jake's phone had gone dead.

Beast Hunter

When Jacob spots a crocodile in the old
quarry, nobody will believe him! He needs to
get a photo as proof before anyone will listen
to him. And that means hunting the beast
himself…

ISBN 978-1-4081-4265-3
RRP £5.99

Run, Jimmy, Run

Jimmy can't stand Dax's bullying any longer. He steals £150 from his father and runs away. But Dax is on the same train – and he sees the money. Now Jimmy and Dax are locked in a frantic chase. Can Jimmy run fast enough and far enough?

ISBN 978-1-4081-4259-2
RRP £5.99

Death Match

While the Nazis occupied Ukraine, Dynamo Kiev's footballers played matches as FC Start. Start won, again, and again. Until they faced a German army side, under the threat of death if they didn't let the occupiers win…

ISBN 978-1-4081-4263-9
RRP £5.99